Alexander Winchell

Adamites and Preadamites

Alexander Winchell

Adamites and Preadamites

ISBN/EAN: 9783337366865

Printed in Europe, USA, Canada, Australia, Japan

Cover: Foto ©Andreas Hilbeck / pixelio.de

More available books at **www.hansebooks.com**

A Popular Discussion

• CONCERNING

The Remote Representatives of the Human Species and their Relation to the Biblical Adam.

—BY—

ALEXANDER WINCHELL, LL.D.,

Professor of Geology and Zoölogy in Syracuse University, and of Historical Geology and Zoölogy in the Vanderbilt University,

[Originally published in the *Northern Christian Advocate.*]

Adamites and Preadamites.

CHAPTER I.

A SAGACIOUS DUTCHMAN.

In 1655 a small book appeared in Paris, which had for its title the unheard-of subject, "Pre-Adamites." It was written in Latin, and its full title was as follows: *Præ-Adamitæ, sive Exercitatio super Versibus duodecimo, decimo tertio et decimo quarto, capitis quinti Epistolæ D. Pauli ad Romanos, quibus inducuntur Primi Homines ante Adamum conditi.*" The book appeared anonymously; and those acquainted with the spirit of the dominant ecclesiasticism of that date will readily divine the motive of its author. It very soon became known, however, that it was written by La Peyrere, a Dutch ecclesiastic, whose name when Latinized was Peyrerius. The work was an attempt to prove from biblical authority that men must have lived on the earth before Adam. Within a year appeared its complement, from the pen of the same author, in which the whole subject was newly argued and more thoroughly discussed. This was a "Theological System based on the Hypothesis of Pre-Adamites." The two works may now occasionally be found in one volume. The Syracuse University possesses a copy.

The following year a book appeared in London, the title of which is a literal translation of that of " Præ-Adamitæ," but it includes also the "Systema Theologicum " of Peyrerius.

In the undeveloped stage of scientific inquiry existing two and a quarter centuries ago, it is certain that no investigation respecting Pre-Adamites could have been conducted on true anthropological principles. In Europe the Bible was the source and basis of all belief. Whatever the ecclesiastical authorities had accepted and sanctioned was held to be taught by the Bible. Whatever the ecclesiastical authorities did not understand the Bible to teach was denounced as heresy. The meaning of the Bible was extracted according to the canons of grammar. There are doctors high in authority amongst us at this day, who maintain that grammatical structure and Hebrew usage are sufficient to light the way to the meaning of the darkest passages of revelation. I suppose a knowledge of Hebrew history and usages is admitted to shed its light upon interpretation, because the text is generally occupied with Jewish affairs. But the inspired writers have sometimes plunged into the midst of the profound and mysterious facts of science : why not, then, summon *all our knowledge* to the task of evoking the meaning of the text? I maintain, against the narrow and pernicious dogma that the Bible is sufficient everywhere to interpret itself, that, on the contrary, it was ordained to be interpreted under the concentrated light of all the learning which has been created by a God-given intelligence in man. I believe that the Bible was written for all time, and that its meaning is so deep and so rich that the accumulated learning of the latest generation of men will be unable to exhaust it.

Not so the contemporaries of Peyrerius. Even where two or more different meanings of the text were equally grammatical and legitimate, that was held to be the true meaning which accorded best with current beliefs. An alternative interpretation, when once promulgated, was held to be divine truth, as absolute and authoritative as if no other interpretation were possible. Perhaps the well-established infallibility of the church had an interest in consistency. No matter if it concerned a fact of a purely scientific or secular character, the verdict was held as binding on the conscience as if the church had been in possession of all possible science.

According to the evidence till then available for the formation of opinion, it had been held that Adam was absolutely " the first being that could be called a man ; " and that he was created in the possession of a culture such as we call enlightened. From time immemorial, biblical scholars had understood this to be the meaning of Genesis. It was, therefore, only on biblical grounds that Peyrerius based the new doctrine of Pre-Adamites. St. Paul was held to teach the existence of men before Adam, in the 12th, 13th and 14th verses of the 5th chapter of his epistle to the Romans, ("Wherefore, as by one man sin entered into the world," etc)

Now it is no part of my purpose to exhibit the scriptural argument on one side or the other. Many of my readers can do that better than I. My purpose is to bring forward certain scientific facts having a bearing on that question, and to leave exegesis to summon these important facts legitimately to its aid. But the writings of Peyrerius possess, in the present status of science, an extraordinary interest. He was the first to promulgate to the world the idea of Pre-Adamites. The first enunciator of the idea was prompted only by biblical considerations, and he has given at least an outline of the scriptural argument in support of the hypothesis. Few of my readers intelligently interested in a question deemed by some so fundamental in a theological system have access to the original work ; and still fewer would have the patience to decipher, as I have done, the quaint old Latin text. I assume, then, that they will consider it a favor to be put in possession of the learned Dutchman's "points." They are as follows :

1. The "one man " (Romans v. 12,) by whom "sin entered into the world " was Adam ; for, in v. 14, that sin is called "Adam's transgression "; therefore "the law " (v. 13) signifies the law given to Adam—natural law, not that given to Moses. 3. The phrase "until the law " (v. 13) implies a time before the law—that is, before Adam ; and, as "sin was in the world " during that time, there must have been men in existence to commit sin. 4. The sin committed before the enactment of the natural law was "material," "actual;" the sin existing after Adam, and through him, was "imputed," "formal," "legal," "adventitious " and "after the similitude of Adam's transgression." 5. Death entered into the world before Adam ; but it was because of the imputation "backwards " of Adam's prospective sin ; and this was necessary, that all men might partake of the salvation provided in Christ. Nevertheless, death before Adam did not "reign." Death was robbed

of its sting. 6. Adam was the "first man" only in the same
sense as Christ was the "second man;" for Adam "was the fig-
ure of Christ." (v. 14.) 7. All men are of one blood in the
sense of one substance —one "matter." The Jews are descended
from Adam; the Gentiles from Pre-Adamites. The first chapter
of Genesis treats of the origin of the Gentiles; the second, of the
origin of the Jews. The Gentiles were created aborigines, in the
beginning, by the "word" of God, in all lands; Adam, the
father of the Jews, was formed of "clay," by the "hand" of God.
Genesis, after the first chapter, is a history, not of the first men,
but of the first Jews. 8. The existence of Pre-Adamites is also
indicated in the biblical account of Adam's family, especially of
Cain, who found a wife amongst some older peoples, and went
forth in fear of violence from strange hands. 9. The biblical
doctrine is corroborated by the evidence afforded by the "monuments" of Egypt and Chaldea; and by the history of the
astronomy, astrology, theology and magic of the Gentiles; as
well as by the racial features of remote and savage tribes; and
by those discoveries of fossil remains in the rocks, which were
then recent events, but which have since become the founda-
tion of the modern science of geology. 10. Hence the epoch
of the creation of the world does not date from that "beginning" commonly figured in Adam, but "from a remoter beginning,
which is to be sought in ages long since passed." 11. The deluge
of Noah was not universal, and it destroyed only the Jews. Nor
is it possible to trace to Noah the origins of all the races of men.

Some of these positions were far in advance of the age; and it
is only just to say that they were defended with learning and in-
genuity, and, best of all, with moderation and candor. But they
were all "heretical." Peyrerius was, therefore, made a victim of
the intolerance of the times. Numerous replies were thrown upon
the world, in most of which, bitterness, contempt and denuncia-
tion were employed to supply all deficiencies of argument. Many
of these I have been able, through the kindness of Mr. Spofford,
Librarian to Congress, to examine in the Congressional Library.
The most important, whose translated titles I here present, will
serve to convey an idea of the temper of the age.

1. "No Pre-Adamite Being; or a Confutation of a certain emp-

ty dream, in which a certain anonymous author, under pretext of sacred Scripture, has lately attempted to impose on the incautious, pretending that men were in the world before Adam."

2. "Animadversions on the Book of Pre-Adamites, in which a late writer is confuted, and the doctrine is defended that Adam was the first of all men."

3. "Response to a treatise entitled Pre-Adamites."

The writers of these responses have, of course, employed strictly scriptural arguments, but they have brought to their aid the dialectic skill which characterized the scholastic theology, as well as the authority of the older writers and the dicta of councils and ecclesiastics.

Now, the whole controversy concerns a question of fact, and we are at this day in possession of many collateral lines of evidence to place by the side of old scriptural interpretation. We can summon ethnology, archæology and anthropology to bear witness. The truth seems to be that these witnesses are quite as competent to testify as witnesses need to be. It is their business to know all that is knowable about the matter. The answer to the question is a fact of science, sustaining fixed relations to the other facts patent before the eyes of the investigator. Whether the world has been populated by people who spread from Ararat forty-two centuries ago, or even from Mesopotamia fifty-nine centuries ago, is a question of fact, to be investigated strictly on the basis of scientific evidence. I think a great deal of evidence is now accessible, perhaps enough to lead us to a final conclusion. Whatever conclusions may be found to represent the truth, I believe our sacred records will be found in harmony.

CHAPTER II.

DISPERSION OF THE NOACHITES.

In discussing the question of Pre-Adamites from anthropological data, the first requisite is to trace the geographical dispersion of the descendants of Noah. The oldest document available for information on this subject is the Book of Genesis; and, aside from any claim to inspiration, its statements respecting the immediate posterity of Noah have been found so closely accordant

with the observed facts, that ethnologists are content to adopt its
information as a starting point. It is agreed, then, that the enlightened nations of the world belong to one race. This is the
race of white men. By Blumenbach it was styled Caucasian,
because our earliest knowledge of the race finds it in the region
south of the Caucasus, and the dominant European family, which
is the leading type of the race, is first discovered on the north
and south of the Caucasus But recent ethnologists designate the
white race as " Mediterranean," because the three families which
constitute it have always, since very early times, dwelt around the
shores of the Mediterranean.

From the earliest history of this race, it has presented three
family types. Since the dispersion of these three families accords
with the biblical account of the dispersion of the posterity of the
three sons of Noah, science has agreed to designate them Hamites,
Semites and Japhetites. The last are more frequently known as
Indo-Europeans or Aryans—names which associate the natives of
India with the dominant European family.

Now, fortunately, we are able to indicate, with considerable
certainty, the regions occupied by the three families of Noachites.
The Hamites are known to have distributed themselves through
the north of Africa, the Nile-valley, and the east of the continent
as far as the straits of Bab-el-Mandeb. They passed from Asia
Minor into the south-east of Europe as early as 2500 B. C., and
occupied the peninsula of Greece under the name of Pelasgians.
To this family belonged the Etruscans, who, at a later date, migrated from Greece and founded a kingdom in Italy, centuries
before the building of Rome by another family. The Phœnicians
were probably Hamites, instead of Semites. Unexpected and
truly wonderful evidence of the common origin of these earliest
Greeks, early Phœnicians and early Egyptians has been unearthed
by Di Cesnola on the island of Cyprus, where pottery and works
of art presenting Egyptian and Phœnician characteristics are
mingled with conceptions characteristically Greek. Late researches have shown that the original Chaldean monarchy also
(before the 18th century B. C.) was Hamitic and not Semitic, and
its written language was Accadian, the parent of the cuneiform
character. These are the views of the latest and best recognized

authorities—Rawlinson, Lenormant, Oppert, Peschel, Jubainville. The Egyptians were certainly pure Hamites, and they are still represented by the Fellaheen, or peasantry of the lower Nile; and especially by the Coptic Christians of the towns. The Hamitic Berbers, including Libyans, Moors, Numidians and Gœtulians are spread, intermingled with Semites and Europeans, through the countries of the Mediterranean, and through the Sahara. Other Hamitic nations, possessing a civilization far beyond that of any of the purely black races, occupy some of the regions about the Nile, especially in Nubia, and are scattered in distinct tribes, united by common linguistic elements, through Abyssinia, and in one direction as far as the heart of Africa, from eight degrees north to three degrees south, and in the other direction, from near Bab-el-Mandeb to Juba on the Indian ocean. The Hamitic dialects and Hamitic civilization, wherever they occur, are readily recognized as superior to any of the indigenous productions of the black races.

The antiquity of Hamitic civilization in Egypt is indicated by the recorded observations of the heliacal rising of the Dog Star. This is the rising of the Dog Star just before the sun, in the first *thoth* or month of the year. This is a conjunction which occurs only once in 1461 years We have a heliacal rising recorded for 1322 B. C. The period, or Sothis, ending at that date began 2782 B. C. As the observations must, apparently, have extended through at least one preceding sothic period, to enable them to know its length, the Egyptian observations must have begun as early as 4243 B. C. This is the opinion of Lepsius (*Chronologie der Aegypter* pt. I. p. 165 seq.) Some other respectable authorities—as Lane, Poole, Brown and Wilkinson—dissent from the inference of so high an antiquity for the first Egyptian dynasty. They maintain that the "era of Menes" reaches back no farther than 2717 B. C.; and some second-hand Egyptologists would bring it down to 2464 B. C. It is impossible to discern the logic, if we could discover the motive, for the prevalent desire to cut down the period of Egyptian civilization, since nearly all the original investigators agree in assigning to it a high antiquity. The most moderate of the German authorities places Menes at 3892 B. C.; and "in his time the Egyptians had long been architects, sculptors, painters, mythologists and theologians." Brugsch (in *Histoire d' Egypte*) has given a chronological canon, in accordance with which the reign of Menes would fall in the years 4455—4395, B. C., and this is in accord with Lepsius. (See also McClintock and Strong's *Cyclopedia*, and Hardwick's *Christ and other Masters*, p. 426, etc.) A similar result is obtained from very elaborate investigations respecting the rate of accumulation of Nilotic deposits. The question of Egyptian antiquity has no relevancy in this discussion; but we deem it a fact of interest that the posterity of Ham, first in the history of the human species, made a record of themselves capable of withstanding the ravages of all time. It is proper also to add that, in spite of English and American incredulity, all the recent archæological discoveries, whether in Egypt, in Assyria, at Hissarlik, Mycenæ or Cyprus, tend to prolong antiquity, and, so far as Egypt is concerned, to strengthen the authority of much suspected and much slighted Manetho. (See Bayard Taylor's *Egypt and Iceland :* Schliemann's *Ancient Troy*, and *Mycenæ ;* Di Cesnola's *Cyprus :* George Smith's *Assyrian Excavations*.)

This is the whole of the geographical dispersion of the Hamites. The reader will note particularly that they have not spread over most parts of Africa. The Negroes are not regarded by modern ethnologists as the descendants of Ham.

Now let us follow the track of the Semites. From the earliest records, they have inhabited western Asia. Thence they have taken possession of parts of eastern Africa. They are represented by the Jews, Arabs, Abyssinians and Aramæans. They subjugated the Hamitic Babylonians and Chaldeans at a date earlier than the migration of Abraham from "Ur of the Chaldees." They adopted the Hamitic religion, which, in western Asia, was the worship of God under the names of Baal and Bel. They probably also conquered, and consolidated with themselves, the Phœnician people. They have migrated, to some extent, into eastern and northern-central Africa, and have familiarized the Negroes with a rude Moslem civilization. The facility with which they had intercourse with the Egyptians and affiliated with the primitive Babylonians and Chaldeans evinces their close affinity with the Hamites. The results, also, of linguistic study show that the Hamites and Semites developed their languages in a common primeval home. This is also taught in Genesis (chap. x, 1:15) where (Semitic) Sidon is described as the oldest son of Canaan, who was descended from Ham. This is the extent of the early migrations of the Semites. They have not escaped observation. They have been conspicuous actors in the historic world.

It only remains to follow the track of the Japhetites, Indo-Europeans or Aryans. When first known, they are national neighbors of the Asiatic Hamites and Semites. They dwelt along the slopes of the Caucasus, and through the gorge of Dariel, within reach of both the Euxine and the Caspian seas. According to some of the authorities, they dwelt nearer to central Asia. Their migrations were both southeastward and eastward. In the first direction, they passed over the Hindu Kush mountains, on the northwestern border of Hindustan, and settled in the region of the "Seven Rivers"—the modern Punjab. Here Brahmanism underwent its development and decline. The Vedas they had brought with them from central Asia. These had originated as early as 1400 to 2400 B. C. Moving still farther southward they displaced an aboriginal population, and drove them to the hills, and to the extreme parts of the Indian peninsula. To this day, Hindustan is populated by the millions of descendants of the Asiatic branch of the Aryan family.

But while these eastward migrations were in progress, another branch of the Aryans moved toward Europe. According to some of the authorities, they passed through the gorge of Dariel into Europe; according to others, they moved along the eastern border of the Caspian Sea. According to all authorities, they appeared in Europe on the north of the Caucasus. Holding communication across the mountains with both Semites and Hamites, they received from them the excellencies of their civilization. From them were obtained wheat, rye and barley; and these cereals, together with the plough and the metals—gold, silver and bronze—they bore with them into central Europe, where they appeared about 2000 B. C.; reached the Adriatic (as Istrians,) and (as Venetes) founded the city of Venice (Venetia). They also held part of the Archipelago; and, as Phrygians, conquered parts of Asia Minor. The Ligurians (including Siculi) dispossessed the Iberians of most of western Europe, at about the same date, and in the time of Hesiod (850 B. C.) they held Gaul. In the sixth century B. C. they also held possession of Spain for eighty years.

Next is the Aryan group composed of the ancestors of the Hellenes, Italians and Kelts. The Hellenic Achæans were in the Peloponnesus in the 14th century B. C., according to Egyptian monuments. They came into Greece by following the eastern coast of the Adriatic southward. Hence they must probably be regarded as an offshoot of the Thracian-group. Continuing eastward, they occupied the Ionian Islands. " By these were the isles of the Gentiles divided in their lands." Later they appeared in Thessaly, and in the 11th century B. C. they had returned to Asia and established settlements upon the coast of Asia Minor. The Ombro-Latins wrested most of Italy from the Ligurians, but were, in turn, subjugated by the Etruscans. Subsequently they regained possession. The Kelts or Gauls suddenly appeared along the valley of the upper Danube, driven, probably, by the Scythians, from the region of the Dnieper. In the 7th and 6th centuries B C., they spread over Gaul, displacing the Ligurians, and passed to the British Islands, where, as Irish and Scotch, they have retained a foothold to this day. At the beginning of the 5th century B. C. they wrested a great part of Spain from the Phœnicians and their Iberian vassals. In the beginning of the 4th century B. C. they extended their authority over the north of Italy and other regions to the Danube and the Black Sea.

The third group belonging to the first Aryan migration into Europe consisted of Slavs and Germans. We first know them as subjects of the Scythians, about 400 B. C. The German stock became differentiated about 182 B. C. under the name of Bastarnians.

A second wave of Indo-Europeans swept from Asia across the European border about 1500 B.C. Under the name of Scythians they seized upon the country bordering on the Dnieper, expelling the Kelts who now proceeded on their conquest of Europe.

Such, in bold outline, is a sketch of Aryan migrations both eastward and westward. In the original site of this family the Iranians still maintain a foothold. From this centre the Brah-

manic people spread over India. From this centre a succession
of waves of migration tended toward Europe. The first of these
we may designate the Thracian; the second, the Hellenic; the
third, the Keltic; the fourth, the Scythian. Probably, however,
the first three migrations were only ramifications of the first Asiatic
invasion, while the Scythians made an independent invasion from
Asia.

The facts here set forth are supplied by the very latest ethnological researches. (See Jubainville, *Les Premiers Habitans de
l'Europe*, 1877, and Le Hon, *L'Homme Fossile*, 1877.) It is of
interest to us to note that the Hindus are members of the same
race, and of the same family of that race, as ourselves. They are
possessed, then, of similar intellectual and moral characteristics.
If we style them "heathen" we must remember that they are
wise and thoughtful heathens, armed with science and philosophy
far above our contempt.

As to the movements of the Aryan family since the Christian
era, history is able to speak with a certain sound. No fragment
of the family has escaped observation. It would not be possible
to conceal itself in the remotest quarters of the world. The
color of its skin would betray it. The tint and texture of its
hair would reveal it. The very speech of the rudest peasant
would proclaim it. The clang and tone of the Greek and the
Sanscrit are in the speech of the most ignorant Suabian and the
most servile Slav.

CHAPTER III.

THE BLACK RACES NOT ADAMITES.

We have traced the sons of Noah in all their wanderings over
the earth. We have swept over Southern and Eastern Asia. We
have pursued the swarms of men across the north and northeast
of Africa. We have followed wave after wave over the Caucasus
and over the Bosphorus; and have seen all Europe, save Northern Russia and Scandinavia, trod by the feet of Asiatic immi-
grants. "These are the families of the sons of Noah, after their
generations in their nations."

But now we reach an interesting juncture in the progress of

our discussion. These Noachites everywhere found older people in possession of the land. Who were they? In central Asia they bordered on the Mongolians—who were they? On the south of the Hindu-Kush they drove before them, to the confines of the peninsula, the aboriginal Dravidians—who were they? In Greece, the Hamitic Pelasgians drove out the cave-dwelling Cyclopes—who were they? In Italy and Spain the Aryan Ligurians found and expelled the Iberians—who were they? Everywhere, Iberians, Ligurians, Achæans, Ombro-Latins, Kelts and Scythians found a people who dwelt in caves, used stone implements and clothed themselves in the skins of beasts—who were they?

These aborigines were everywhere people whom we cannot trace to the sons of Noah. Between Adam and Noah's flood was an interval of 1656 years. Could these unknown peoples have ramified from the stock of Adam during that interval? Let us look in their faces and see if we can detect any affinity with the recognized sons of Adam.

There, first, was the Dravidian race, dispossessed of the peninsula of India by the eastern branch of the Aryan family. They remain distinct to the present day, and their characteristics agree with the representations which have been made of them from time to time in the progress of history. Their skins are dark; their hair is black and curly; their lips are intumescent, but their jaws are *not* prognathous, like those of the Negroes. They still hold possession of a belt along the east coast of Hindustan, and even stretch far into the interior. They also retain a foothold upon the west coast, and linger in Beloochistan. The northern half of Ceylon is also the seat of a numerous Dravidian population. One of their languages is the Tamul or Tamil, spoken by ten millions of people, and the repository of an ancient literature of surprising richness. These people are *not* the descendants of Noah. We may assume, however, that they are not so divergent from the types of the Noachian race as to preclude the admission that they may be descended from the same Adam. Let us grant that they may be Adamites.

What shall we say of the Mongoloids? This vast race, forming two-thirds the population of the globe, spreads over all eastern and northern Asia and Arctic Europe. It possesses the Japanese islands, and many other islands of Polynesia. The

Chinese and Tartars and Malays belong here, as well as the Siberian tribes, and the' Finns and Lapps of Europe. The fierce Huns were of this race; and so, with more or less of intermixture, are the modern Magyars and Turks. More than this, the aborigines of America are Mongoloids—not less the civilized Peruvians and Aztecs than the Chippeways, Iroquois and other North American tribes, and the Aleuts and Eskimo of the extreme north. The Mongoloids encircle the globe. They belt it without interruption, in the frozen latitudes; and the Mongoloid Malays penetrate the tropics of Polynesia, while Mongoloid Americans range through all the zones. No race, save the Mediterranean, has ever had a dispersion at all comparable. Can these be cousins of the Noachites, and brethren of the Dravida? Are these the sons of Adam? The dusky Dravida could not well disown relationship, on the score of complexion, with the dusky Malay. But the Dravidian's curly hair reveals little affinity with the straight, coarse hair of the Mongoloid; and the latter's high cheek bones and generally obliquely set eyes wedge the races apart so far that we feel a little incredulity respecting the claim that the antediluvian period of less than two thousand years could have marked them with such disparity, while the two thousand years of our acquaintance with the two races has witnessed no sensible divergence. Could 1656 years differentiate three races, while the next 4225 years have not increased the number? Must the Mongoloids be admitted as Adamites? Since we have provisionally let in the dusky Dravida, let us also admit provisionally the dusky Mongoloids, and then ascertain what results.

The Negroes are about to cause us trouble. The Negroes have made us a great deal of trouble. The whole group of black races recedes from the white and dusky races. These tropical ebonites are now regarded as comprising four races. The three families of Noachites constitute still, after a lapse of more than four thousand years, but a single race. Compare with this fact the differentiation of black men into four properly characterized races, and we have at once a fact bearing on the antiquity of the black races. These races are (1) Negroes, (2) Hottentots and Bushmen, (3) Papuans, (4) Australians. Besides their black skins, they all have narrow heads (*dolicho-cephalous*—a term which

means long heads, but they are only relatively long, because so
thin) and projecting jaws (*prognathous*). They possess long thigh-
bones, and sometimes, also long arms. The shanks are lean, the
pelvis is obliquely set, and the secondary sexual characters are
deficient. The Negroes are further distinguished by short,
crisped hair, each fibre of which is flattened, like the fibre of
wool. The beard is almost wanting, the lips are thick, the forehead is retreating, the nose flattened. But why describe the Negro? The home of the Negro is all Africa from the southern
border of the Sahara to the country of the Hottentots and Bushmen—except some portions on the extreme east which have been
possessed by the Hamites, as before stated. The northern tribes
are the Soudan Negroes, and embrace numerous peoples speak-
ing many different languages and dialects, and stretching quite
to the interior of the continent. The southern tribes are the
Bantus, and embrace the Zanzibar and Mozambique nations,
and the well known Betchuans and Kaffirs connected with the
missionary labors of Livingstone and Moffat.

All the southern portion of the African continent belongs to
the Hottentots and Bushmen. They have a leathery brown skin,
which becomes greatly wrinkled with age; and their hair is pecu-
liarly matted in tufts. This does not result from ignorance of
combs and brushes. The Hottentots—or Koi-Koin, as they call
themselves—have sometimes been placed at the foot of the anthropological scale; but this is unjust, as they have very distinct
religious ideas, know how to work iron, and possess a language
so complete, and marked by such affinities with the Egyptian,
that many investigators—Moffat, Lepsius, Pruner Bey, Max Mul-
ler, Whitney and Bleek—have turned our thoughts to the inquiry,
whether the Egyptians and the Hottentots have decended from
a common stock since the development of language, or have
simply lived in contact with each other at some former period.

We turn now to the Papuans and Australians. The former
inhabit New Guinea and the other islands of Micronesia, including the Fiji archipelago. Their matted and tufted hair stands
out wildly from their heads in shaggy crowns six or eight inches
in height. The beard is abundant, and the skin ranges from
dark chocolate color to blue-black. The jaws are less projecting

than in the Negro, and the nose, instead of being flat, is broad and straight, and sometimes even aquiline. In intelligence, they range from the besotted fetish-worshipers of New Guinea, to the semi-civilized Fijians.

The Australians are so named from the vast island, which, with Tasmania and small contiguous islands, is their exclusive home. Their whole body is thickly hairy. The hair of the head is matted and shaggy, but less spreading than that of the Papuans. Their language is well developed, and the use of the boomerang is another proof of their intellectual capacity. So is their system of religious beliefs and practices. But they use no metallic implements, and their boats are mere logs, which may be regarded as the initial point in the evolution of naval structures.

These four constitute the Black races. We have to consider whether they, too, are descendants of the same Adam as the White and Dusky races. Let us begin with the purely linguistic method, which refuses to invoke collateral aids according to any consistent system, for eliciting the meaning of Scriptural language. Adam is a word which signifies *red*. The man thus designated must have had at least some infusion of red in his complexion. We can readily discover this tint in the skin of the white man. Before the invention of clothing, the summer sun upon the plains of central Asia must have developed in the white man's skin a very visible amount of ruddiness. It is admitted on all hands that the Adam of the Bible was the progenitor of the White race. But now, can the same term be applied to those races which I have designated " Dusky "? The Bible gives no distinct account of the genealogy of these races showing that their progenitor was "red." It is only popular opinion which traces them, with all other men, to the white man's Adam. But as we have assumed that they may, on anthropological principles, be admitted as Adamites, so we may admit that the term "Adam" is capable of sufficient stretching to cover the dusky Mongoloids and Dravida. Is it now thought the word will bear still a farther stretch? My private judgment forbids. I can discover some red in the complexion of the Mediterranean stock, and even in that of the Mongolian and Dravidian; but when you tell me that the Negro has

3

a color which the old Hebrew would have called "red," I feel myself very ignorant of the meaning of terms.

Anthropologically, color possesses less significance than the meaning of the term Adam. It is confessedly one of the less constant characteristics of race. But the strict interpretation of Scripture is very often insisted on, and in this case I would like to pin the strict constructionists to their chosen method; because the strict construction, as will be shown, is the one which corresponds with the entire range of facts.

CHAPTER IV.

THE NEGRO PREADAMIC.

In the attempt to ascertain whether the biblical Adam was the progenitor of all mankind, or only of the White and Dusky races, I pointed out the fact that literal interpretation renders the name Adam inapplicable to races whose complexion displays no noticeable tinge of "red." But in the attempt to make Adam the father of the Black races, I find myself beset by other and graver difficulties. The Adam of Genesis is supposed to date from an epoch less than two thousand years before Noah. There have been almost six thousand years for the posterity of Adam to attain their present amount of divergence, as exemplified in different families and races of man. This has not perceptibly increased since the Christian era. I suppose all will admit, on the evidence of history and monuments, that the Semitic, Hamitic and Aryan features were not perceptibly less marked two thousand years ago than at present. If any one doubts this, he can be easily satisfied by turning over the pages of any work illustrated from the monuments of Egypt and Assyria. (For accessible American digests, see Nott and Gliddon's *Types of Mankind and Indigenous Races of the Earth*.) Better, let him visit the Assyrian and Egyptian departments of the Louvre and the British and Berlin Museums. It is equally true that delineations of Negro features, executed at a date not less remote, are exactly as pronounced as the realities of to-day. Now, I think we may fairly take 2,000 years as the measure of 4,000. If these races and families have not sensibly diverged in 2,000 years, will the reader believe that all the marked divergence which actually exists took place during the previous 4,000 years?

But the negative argument is much stronger. The Egyptian and Assyrian monuments which testify to the distinctness of races and families date back one or two thousand years farther than our era. In these sculptures and mural paintings the stately Semite with his aquiline nose is instantly distinguished from the nimble Hamite with his straight nose, full lips and oblique and languishing eyes. Amongst the other figures the Negro is often discovered by his thick lips, projecting jaws and wooly hair. For at least half of the recognized interval between Adam and us, the Negro has been a Negro; the Hamite, a Hamite; the Semite, a Semite. Archæology and ethnology, therefore, force this alternative conclusion upon us: If human beings have existed but 6,000 years, then the different races had *separate beginnings*, as Agassiz long since maintained—each race in its own geographical area. But if all human beings are descended from one stock, then the starting point was *more than 6,000 years back;* as Huxley and the evolutionists generally maintain; and the Duke of Argyll and other anti-evolutionists equally maintain. Accordingly, if the reader insist that Adam was absolutely the first creature which could be called a man, he must admit first that "red," in Hebrew, means "black," and secondly, that the biblical chronology between Adam and Noah omits at least nine-tenths of the time. In such an admission, he will have the excellent company of the Duke of Argyll, (*Primeval Man*).

Now, every person remains free to contemn a logical difficulty, and commiserate the unfortunate facts for being opposed to his belief. But my training has been such that logic and facts still command a degree of respect. Nor am I enough of an actor to play the part of an idiot. If I can avoid a difficulty I shall not dash out my brains against it. Let us consider Adam the father of the White and Dusky races. These, then, are Adamites; and have a chronology extending back about 6,000 years—perhaps all the time we require. The Black races, then, are preadamites; and there is no objection to allowing all the time requisite for their divergence from some common stock. This view recognizes the unity of man; the possession of "one blood" by all the races, one moral and intellectual nature, and one destiny; it recognizes Adam as the progenitor of the nations which form the theme of biblical history; it explains sundry biblical allusions and implications—for instance, the wife found by Cain in the land of Nod; Cain's fear of violence from others when condemned to the life of a "fugitive and a vagabond;" the antithesis of the "sons of God" and the "daughters of men;" it validates the biblical chronology; it satisfies the demands of facts. The only objection outstanding against this view is the authority of an opinion formed two or three thousand years ago, by men who also held the opinion that witches ride broomsticks through the air, and that the stars were created two days before Adam, though some of them are so distant that their light has been a hundred thousand years in reaching us.

Now, let us take up another set of considerations. The Adam of our race is generally regarded, I believe, as a man with natural endowments as good as our own. At least, I shall claim so much for him. His immediate posterity developed all the intelligence and moral characteristics which could be expected of modern men similarly situated, and having absolutely everything to learn. If the same Adam must be regarded the progenitor of the Black races, then these races represent a wide-spread degeneracy, which is not only vast and appalling, but must be pronounced eminently improbable. Now, degeneracy of tribes and fragments of tribes is a phenomenon quite familiar in anthropology. It has taken place where the oppression of superior tribes has driven the weaker into the midst of conditions unfriendly to existence. The Spaniards crushed the spirit out of the Peruvians and the Aztecs. The miserable Fuegians are crowded to the dripping and stormy and inhospitable shores of Cape Horn, where nature begrudges man a stick of fuel, and a crab's claw is a thanksgiving feast. The timid Andamaners are the persecuted remnant of a race driven to the shelters of the mountains, and tormented by the penal colony which England has planted on their lands. The Dyaks of Borneo, skulking in the mountains and jungles of the interior, are despised by the superior border tribes of their own race, and denied a rightful place in the ranks of humanity. Some of the Congo tribes which inhabit the pestilential regions of the west coast of Africa have been degenerated to the last degree. Only the most sluggish natures escape the fatal infection of miasm; and, hence, only the most brutish survive to perpetuate their race. By a process of natural selection, the law of progress is reversed. The law of *progress*, I say, for it is a *real* law of the organic world. Should it be claimed that the white man's Adam had descended from a common stock with the Negro, all nature cries out in assent. But should it be affirmed that the Negro is degenerated from the white man's Adam, every fact in nature shakes its head in denial. The Black man is too numerous. The affirmation would establish a law of retrogression. Progression, I say, is the law. The Black man on the healthful and fertile plateaux of central Africa is not oppressed by miasm, nor starvation, nor cruel neighbors. He is free to roam where he will—like the Digger Indian of North America, or the driveling Botecuda of Brazil. No, these savages exist in a normal condition; they are coming up instead of going down. Their Adam was farther from our Adam than they are. Their long thigh bones, and lean shanks, and projecting jaws are inheritances of a lower, rather than a higher ancestry.

CHAPTER V.

THE NEGRO PREADAMIC,—*Continued*.

The conclusion that the Black races are preadamic is opposed, so far as I know, only on the three following grounds:

I. *The Negroes are supposed to be the descendants of Ham.* This has been the traditional opinion of the Church, and hence of mankind at large. I doubt whether the Church would reach the opinion if the question were now first opened in the light of present knowledge. But because the Church and mankind in general have so long held the opinion, cautious conservatism is reluctant to let go its hold. The opinion, really, is not worthy of scientific consideration. I may summarize the objections to it. 1. Scripture does not sustain the affirmation. 2. We discover the posterity of Ham in the population of Mizraim (Egypt;) and

in the compatriots of Nimrod, the son of Cush, the founder of
Babel and the other Accadian cities; and in the compatriots of
Asshur "who builded Nineveh;" and the compatriots of the Sidians
who were descended from Canaan, the son of Ham. This is the
plain teaching of Genesis, and there is no space for the assumption
that the Negroes represent Ham's posterity. The consequences
of Noah's curse upon Canaan must be traced out in some other
direction. (See M'Causland, *Adam and the Adamites* and *The
Builders of Babel.*) 3. The best ethnological authorities oppose
the view. (See especially Rawlinson, *Herodotus* and *Historical
Evidences.* Also M'Causland, as above. Dr. Whedon has expressed an inclination to agree with M'Causland. See *Methodist
Quarterly Review,* Jan., 1871, p. 153 and July, 1872, p. 526.)
4. The view is opposed by the facts of archæology. The monuments of Egypt display the Negro in a state of complete differentiation at a period little later than the Deluge (2348 B. C.)
The absurdity of supposing that this had been accomplished in
1,500 or 2,000 years is glaring. 5. The view opposes the universal law of progression as I have already explained. 6. It
does not account for the other Black races—Australians and Papuans. Whose sons are they?

II. *The ethnological list given in Genesis is not complete.* Well, if
this is granted, it must tend to help the Negro to an Adamic an-
cestor in one of two ways: 1. It may mean that the several patriarchs named had other posterity than that mentioned; but
this would not help the theory, for *time* is what the case needs,
not more brothers and cousins. 2. It may mean that some of
the generations are omitted, and hence those mentioned do not
cover all the time. Whether such omissions exist, Biblical scholars must decide. Extended time would provide for the whole
amount of the race divergences existing a thousand years before
Christ. But yet two difficulties would remain. These are the
color of Adam's skin and the *degeneracy* of the Negro. This
leads me, then, to the third objection.

III. *The Negro is not inferior to the white man.* To this I
have to reply: 1. If, when the sun is shining brightly, a man
tells me it is dark, I can only pronounce him blind. The inferiority of the Negro is a fact everywhere patent. I imply here

only inferiority of intelligence, the instrument of self-helpfulness and of all civilization. I need not argue the fact; *circumspice*. But when this inferiority is conceded, we always hear the appeal to "unfavorable conditions." This leads me to note, 2. The African continent has always been *favorably* conditioned. In the first place, it had a land connection with Asia and the seats of ancient civilization. It even had a remote civilization planted within its own borders; and the fires of Egyptian civilization have never been extinct; while for two thousand years the enlightenment of Europe has been within accessible distance. In the second place, the salubrity of the climate, the fertility of the soil, the vast hydrographic system of lakes and rivers, have all conspired to give the interior of the continent natural conditions unsurpassed by those of the site of any civilization which ever existed. Thirdly, the indigenous productions of Africa have supplied other conditions of human advancement. There exist two native cereals, Negro millet and Kaffir corn, which supply material for bread. There are the edible "bread-roots" and also "earth-nuts," which are adequate to supply the daily food of whole villages. As to fruit trees, there are the doom-palm, the oil-palm and the "butter tree." Moreover, for thousands of years the way has been open as wide as the continent for the introduction of the cereals of Asia. In fact, they have long been known to the natives; and maize, the manioc root and sugar cane, as well as wheat and barley, have spread far toward the interior. There, too, have been domesticated animals, received, probably, from the Egyptians in a domesticated state ; but no native animal has ever been domesticated. The Aryans of India employed the elephant as a beast of burden; but the African elephant was never utilized. These are not the conditions under which a whole race could be crushed into a process of degeneracy. 3. Comparison with other races shows the Negro's inferiority. The Egyptian civilization was reared on the African continent by the side of the barbarous Negro, and under the same conditions. If the materials of civilization were introduced from Asia, it was certainly easier for the Negro to introduce them from Egypt. America is not naturally superior in its physical conditions to Africa. Its only cereal is maize. Its principal edible roots are the mandioca and the potato; and the feeble llama and vicuna are the only native animals capable of domestication as beasts of burden. Yet the civilization of the Nahuatl nations of Mexico, the Quiches of Central America, the Mayas of Yucatan and the Aymaras and Quichuas of Peru, had become, both in respect to intellectual and industrial advances, and judicial, moral and religious conceptions, almost a stage of true enlightenment. The glaring fact of Negro inferiority in respect to social conditions cannot be explained by any appeal to adverse conditions. Such are the ethnological facts and the co-ordinated circumstances. But in proof of my position I make another point. 5. The anatomical structure of the Negro is inferior. The lean shanks, the prognathous profile, the long arms (which do not always exist) the black skin, the elongated and oblique pelvis— these are *all* characteristics in which, so far as the Negro diverges from the White man, he approximates the African apes. The skull also is inferior in structure and in capacity, and in the relative expansion of its different regions. Among Whites, the relative abundance of " cross-heads " (having permanently unclosed the longitudinal and transverse sutures on the top of the head) is one in seven; among Mongolians, it is one in thirteen; among Negroes it is one in fifty-two. This peculiarity is supposed by some to favor the prolonged development of the brain. In any event, it is most frequent in the highest races. Again, the prevailing form of the Negro head is dolichocephalous; that of civilized races is mesocephalous and brachycephalous. That is, it lacks the breadth which we find associated with executive ability. The broadest Negro skull does not reach the average of the Germans nor does the best Australian skull, let me add, reach the average of the Negro. Finally, the capacity of the Negro cranium is inferior. Assuming 100 as the average capacity of the Australian skull, that of the Negro is 111.6 and that of the Teuton 124.8. Now, no fact is better established than the general relation of intellect to weight of brain. Welker has shown that the brains of 26 men of high intellectual rank surpassed the average weight by 14 per cent. Of course, quality of brain is an equally important factor; and hence not a few men with brains even below the average have distinguished themselves for scholarship.

But this does not abolish the rule; nor does it prove that the racial inferiority of the Negro brain, in respect to size, is not to be taken as an index of racial inferiority in respect to intelligence and the capacity for civilization; and this all the more since the quality of the Negro brain is also inferior.

I am not responsible for the inferiority of the Negro. I am responsible if I ignore the facts. I am culpable if I hold him to the same standard as the White man. My appeals to him must be of a widely different character from my appeals to the Aryan Hindu, or the Mongoloid American savage. The ethnological facts have their application in all missionary efforts.

Nor must these statements be set down to the Negro's demerit. If it would help my argument, I could point out the excellencies and capacities of Negro natures, and would take pleasure in doing so. But this would be irrelevant. I have indicated the proofs of the Negro's physical, intellecual and social *inferiority*. I have insisted on the high improbability of a *degeneracy* from the grade of Adamic races to that of the actual Negro ; and finally I have maintained that if a complete racial degeneracy were admissible, the *time* between the biblical Adam and the date of ancient monuments depicting the fully developed Negro, is palpably insufficient for the racial divergence.

— —

CHAPTER VI.

SCHEME OF PREHISTORIC TIMES.

In previous chapters, I have indicated reasons for holding that the black races are probably preadamic. I have no doubt that some who have paid these pages the compliment of an attentive perusal have felt a little discomforted at the announcement of such a conclusion. Such views, they think, are calculated to disorganize belief—old and hitherto unassailed belief. Such a result may not be an unmitigated evil. The disorganization of an old belief may be wholly advantageous. Some beliefs need to be disorganized. Built like rude log cabins, in a primeval period, they ought to be taken down as soon as we are able to build better. I have a reverence for old beliefs: but I think they ought

4

to be preserved as relics. What has become of the primitive shanty in this City of Salt? Did anybody refuse to pull it down because it was old? I venture the assertion that the spirit of the age has not even preserved it as a relic. For the old shanties of opinion, which have been a refuge for the ignorance of the past, I have a sentimental regard; but I am not willing to continue to skulk beneath them, when I see the stars through all the roof, and find the sills eaten up by rats.

Allow me to indicate the superstructure of a modern belief, and, therefore, a belief better co-ordinated with the present conditions of human knowledge. Do not. think me laying corner stones; they have been laid by Moses; they have been laid by Champollion, and Lepsius, and Sir William Jones, and the Rawlinsons, and Haug, and Max Müller, and George Smith; they have been laid by philologists and archæologists and ethnologists; by zoölogists and geologists, and by interpreters of our sacred histories. I build on such foundations, and the reader shall see if the new edifice is not fairer than the old.

It was many thousand years ago that the first being appeared which could be called a man. Whether descended from a being unworthy to be called a man, is a collateral question which rests on other foundations. We shall return to it. That first of all men did not make his advent in Asia, nor in Europe, nor in America. He appeared either in Africa or in a continental land which stretched from Madagascar to the East Indies; and which has since become reduced to a few relics of itself. His skin was probably black, and well clothed with hair. He had implanted within him the divine spark of intelligence. He listened to the voice of conscience and felt the claims of duty. If not indigenous in Africa, his descendants took possession of that continent. They spread over Australia and Borneo and the lesser islands of the sea. In the course of thousands of years, they disseminated themselves over considerable portions of Asia.

The time arrived, at length, when, under the law of progressive development, a grade had been reached nearly on a level with that of modern civilized man, in respect to native capacities. Now appeared the founder of the Adamic family. His home was in central Asia. Seth and Cain were either his sons, or nations descended from him. He had also " other sons and daughters " in the same sense. The Sethites and Cainites and the other tribes of Adam, as they spread themselves eastward, displaced and at length exterminated the Preadamites of Asia. They overran the peninsula of Hindustan and extended themselves into Ceylon. Under the influences of climate, and other physical conditions, they diverged from the Adamic aspect, and became Dravidians. The northern or Mongolian (also called Turanian) stream of Adamites was more prolific, and more inspired by the spirit of emigration. Continuing eastward till arrested by the Pacific, the stream divided. The southern branch swarmed over the Malayan peninsula and islands, and dispossessed the Preadamites of many of the islands of Polynesia. The northern branch moved toward Behring's Straits. Here a portion of them passed over the isthmus which then connected Asia and America, and in the course of thousands of years extended to Greenland and Cape Horn. Another portion of the northern branch was reflected westward, and followed the northern slope of the continent into Europe, and overran all Europe.

Meantime a great deluge occurred in western Asia. Whole populations were destroyed. The Adamites who had remained near the original seat of the family were swept out of existence. The vacated regions of western Asia were, for a time, occupied by the wandering Mongoloids. But the descendants of Noah crowded upon them. The Mongoloids, though numerous, were inferior. They passed through the isthmus of Suez, before the settlement of the Hamites in Egypt, and ranged along the south coast of the Mediterranean, crowding the aborigines into the desert. At the Straits of Gibraltar, they crossed over into Spain. The straits were then an isthmus. But they found another outlet. The fabled Atlantis, of which the tradition has been preserved by Plato and Theopompus, has been discovered At least, we have found the remnants of it. It lay along the present bed of the Atlantic from the Bay of Biscay to the mouth of the Niger. The Maderia islands and the Canaries are surviving vestiges of Atlantis. Its worn stump has been traced by the soundings of American and British explorers ; and the outlines of the obliterated continent have recently been mapped in a scientific pub-

lication. (*Nature*, March 1, 1877.)   In Atlantis was reared a
Mongolian monarchy.   Its armies, according to the tradition
said by Plato to have been preserved in a poem by Solon, marched
eastward and subjugated all the region south of the Mediterranean, as far as Egypt.   The valley of the Nile had, by this time,
been populated by Hamites, and they successfully resisted the
encroachments of the Atlantideans.   This was during the reigns
of Cecrops, 1582 B. C., and Erechtheus, 1409 B. C.,—dates preserved by the marble of Paros.

Subsequently the Hamitic Egyptians encroached upon the
Mongolian territory south of the Mediterranean, and at an early
period displaced the Mongoloids from this region and from the
continent of Atlantis.

In the course of time Atlantis was swallowed up by the sea.
Whether sunken by an earthquake shock or slowly gnawed down
by the waves, is matter for conjecture.   A relic of the ancient
population, the Guanches, survived until recently upon the Canaries—the only islands in the Atlantic ocean which were found
occupied by an aboriginal people.   Ethnologists regard them as
belonging to the Berber branch of Hamites.

According to the evidence of skulls, the troglodytes of Europe
were Mongoloids.   They were the earliest population of the continent.   I suppose they descended from that reflected stream of
Mongoloids who impinged against the shores of the Pacific ocean
in their eastward movement, and recrossed Asia along the northern boundary of the region held by the Noachites.   When they
took possession of Europe, the continental glacier was just dis-
solving.   The rivers were flooded with the melting snows.   England was joined to the continent.   The hairy elephant was rang-
ing over Southern Europe.   The two-horned rhinoceros wallowed
in the marshes of France.   The cave-bear was tenanted in the
caverns of the mountains, and the voice of the cave-lion rever-
berated through the aisles of the primeval forest.   This prima-
tive European was purely barbarous.   He usurped the caverns
for his abode.   He fashioned stones into implements of warfare
and set himself about the extermination of the wild beasts.   His
more civilized cousins of the Atlantidean branch of his race made
an early invasion into south-western Europe.   Known to history

as Iberians, they took possession of the Spanish peninsula and
extended their conquests over Italy, Gaul, Sardinia, Corsica and
the British Islands.   The Iberians, in turn, were dispossessed by
immigrations, first, of Hamitic Pelasgians, and, afterward, of
Aryan Illyrians and Ligurians.   In our times, all that remains of
them is the little nation of Basques in the north of Spain and the
south of France ; while the troglodyte stone folk have retreated
along the track of the retreating glaciers, to the borders of the
Arctic ocean and are represented in Europe by the Mongolian
Finns and Lapps.

This scheme of prehistoric times, embracing only a few con-
jectural features, weaves in all the facts of history and science.
If it traverses old opinions, we need not mourn.   New truths are
better than old errors.   Fact is worth more than opinion.   Certainty is more desirable than confidence.   Progressive knowledge
implies much unlearning.   The loss of a belief, like the death of
a friend, seems a bereavement ; but a false belief is only an ene-
my in a friend's cloak.   It is only truth which is divine ; and, if
we embrace an error, we shall not find it ratified in the oracles
of divine truth.   We who hold to the valid inspiration of the
sacred records may feel assured that nothing will be found affirmed therein which collides with the final verdict of intelligence.
Nor has the color of the first man any concern with a simple religious faith.   If our creed embodies a dogma which enunciates
what is really a conclusion, true or false, based on scientific evidence—that is, evidence brought to light by observation and
research—that may be exscinded as an excrescence.   All such
subjects are to be settled by scientific investigation—not by councils of the church.   Ecclesiastical faith has had a sorry experience in the attempt to sanctify popular opinions.   A faith that
has had to surrender the geocentric theory and the denial of an-
tipodes, and of the high geological antiquity of the world, should
have learned to discriminate between religious faiths and scientific opinions.   Religious faith is more enduring than granite.
Scientific opinion is uncertain ; it may endure like granite, or
vanish like a summer cloud.   Religious faith is simple, pure and
incorruptible ; scientific opinion is a compound of all things corruptible and incorruptible.   Let us not adulterate pure faith with

corruptible science. An unadulterated faith can be defended by the sturdiest blows of reason and logic; a corrupt faith puts reason and logic to shame.

CHAPTER VII.

RETROSPECT OF PRIMEVAL MAN IN EUROPE.

According to authentic ethnological evidence, the earliest men in Europe were not Noachites. The descendants of the three sons of Noah, in the progress of their dispersion, found older peoples in possession of Europe, and drove them out. The earliest Noachites known to have settled on that continent were of the family of Hamites. These were subsequently displaced by Aryans. (See second chapter.) The primitive tribes encroached upon by Hamitic immigration were, we have good reason to believe, Mongoloids. (See fifth chapter.) These I have assumed to be Adamites. The primitive Mongoloids seem, at one time, to have spread over the entire continent. Indeed, according to the general positions of this discussion, the Mongoloids and Dravida held possession of the greater part, if not the whole, of Asia, in antediluvian times, and even for some ages subsequently. That some uniform race of men populated the Orient from India to Great Britain, in remote prehistoric times, is evinced by the similarity of the monuments left behind in all the intervening countries. I refer especially to tumuli and huge stone structures of a certain style. That these widely distributed monuments were erected by peoples of antediluvian origin, is proven by the fact that the posterity of Noah, wherever they went, found these monuments already in existence. That these antediluvian people were Mongoloids, is shown: 1. By the forms of some of their skulls and the stature and porportions of their skeletons. 2. By the Mongoloid character of the Samoyedes, Lapps and Finns, who are regarded as the remnants of the primitive population displaced by the families of Noachites. The Basques, another remnant, are not definitely recognized as Mongolian.

What was the condition of those remotely prehistoric peoples? Modern researches have been wonderfully prolific in materials illustrating the physical, intellectual, social, moral and religious status of the earliest inhabitants of Europe ; and the developments of investigation in Asia, as far as pursued, are entirely in accord. Indeed, it may be said that the prehistoric antiquities of America present so many resemblances that archæology confirms the verdict of ethnology, which assigns the aborigines of America to a Mongolian origin in Asia.

The chief sources of information respecting prehistoric man in Europe are, in addition to the traditions preserved in ancient history, the remains of man found in caverns, river drifts, alluvial deposits, volcanic tuff, peat bogs, kitchen middens, tumuli and megaliths, and, finally, the ancient lake dwellings.

Whether primitive men dwelt to any extent in houses of their own construction, it appears, both from history and archæology, that caverns everywhere have served as human shelters. Nor do they seem to have been temporary refuges; for immense quantities of human remains frequently occur in them, imbedded in successive layers of earth, broken stones and stalagmitic material, to the depth of ten or twenty feet. These remains consist chiefly of stone and bone implements. Sometimes ashes and cinders remain; and in front of the celebrated rock shelter of Aurignac are the relics of an ancient stone hearth, on which was cooked the food which probably served as a funeral repast; for within the cave, which had been closed by a large stone, were uncovered the remains of seventeen human beings. It is seldom that the bones of men occur in the caverns, but the bones of the cavebear, hyena and lion, as also those of the reindeer, ox, mammoth, rhinoceros and other animals, are often abundant. No metal seems to have been known to the cave-dwellers.

Other human relics, as ancient as the earliest occupation of the caverns, are found imbedded in the gravel and sand which line certain river valleys in France and England. These deposits were at first supposed to be Glacial or even Tertiary in age ; but it is now admitted that they were formed by the rivers which occupy the valleys, at a time when they flowed at levels thirty to fifty feet higher than at present. It is a doctrine of geology that this stage of the rivers existed at the time when the continental glaciers were melting. The human relics obtained from these gravels are chiefly articles of rough stone and bone. With these are associated some remains of extinct quadrupeds. Some alluvial deposits near Strasburg, and at Maestricht and elsewhere, have afforded rude flints and human bones. In the volcanic mountain of Denise, in Central France, human bones have been found imbedded in volcanic tuff; and in another locality tuff resulting from the same eruption encloses the remains of a cave-hyena and a hippopotamus.

Again the peat-bogs of Denmark have afforded a rich series of relics chronologically arranged. These bogs are from ten to thirty feet deep. In the lowest portions they enclose remains of the scotch fir, a tree no longer growing in Denmark; and with these are associated implements of flint. Above are found traces of the common oak, now very rare in Denmark, and, associated therewith, implements and ornaments of bronze, as well as stone. But in the highest portions of the peat are found the remains of the beechen forest now living, and mingled with these are relics of an age of iron. The bogs of Ireland have been correspondingly productive.

The kitchen-middens, or kitchen refuse heaps, are piles of earth and human relics occurring along the shores of Denmark, reaching sometimes a height of ten feet, with a breadth of 200 and a length of 1,000. They are largely made up of the shells of the oyster, cockle and other edible molluscs, but these are plentifully mingled with the bones of various quadrupeds, birds and fishes, which have served as food. Interspersed with these offal accumulations are flint knives, hatchets and other instruments of stone, horn, wood and bone, with fragments of coarse pottery. No traces of bronze or iron occur. Such refuse heaps lie upon the shores of many other countries, and have been described in America, from Florida to Maine.

The megaliths or huge roughly hewn blocks of stone, arranged in rude structures, abound in nearly all the countries of Europe. Those called "dolmens" are enormous slabs resting horizontally on upright stones. "Menhirs" are huge stone posts, sometimes standing singly, and sometimes surrounding a dolmen, when they constitue what is called a "cromlech." The "dolmens" were for centuries regarded as the stone altars of the ancient

Druids; but we now know that they were as mysterious to the Druids, two thousand years ago, as to ourselves. Sometimes the dolmen is covered by a mound of earth. That these were burial places is proved by the occurrence of skeletons in some of them.' In certain tumulus-dolmens, the crypt inclosed by the stones is divided into several compartments, each enclosing a skeleton. The associated implements are mostly of stone.

The lake dwellings were cabins erected on piles in the lakes of Switzerland and other European countries. Relics of everything connected with the life of the lake-dwellers were, as a matter of course, accumulated in the bottom of the lake around them. In recent times, these have been discovered and dredged up. They consist of such remains as have already been enumerated, with the addition of articles of bronze. They, hence, belonged to a later age. In certain lakes artificial islands were formed of stones and timbers, on which huts were built. In Ireland these are called "crannoges," and are now deeply covered with turf.

The interpretation of these human relics is, of course, greatly helped by the study of modern savages, and the accounts of ancient history. The flint arrow-heads of the American Indian, for instance, are fashioned precisely like some of those found in European caverns and lake-habitations. To understand the ancient lake-dwellings, recall the account by Herodotus of an ancient tribe dwelling in Pæonia, now a part of Roumelia, who erected cabins on piles; and also the narrative by D'Urville of the lake-dwellers of New Guinea. As illustrations of the kitchen-middens, we may turn to the shell-heaps on the north-west coast of Australia, and the city border offal heaps of Guayaquil and Mexico. In India some of the tribes still erect cromlechs. Early historic times also reflect a light on the pre-historic ages. "Jacob took a stone and set it up for a pillar," (Gen. xxxi, 45; see, further, ver. 46-52,) and at Mount Sinai Moses erected twelve pillars—menhirs, (Exod. xxiv, 4; Josh. iv, 21-22.) In connection with tumuli, it may be remembered that Semiramis raised a mound over her husband; stones were piled up over the remains of Laicus: Achilles raised to Patroclus a mound more than 100 feet in diameter; Alexander erected one over the ashes of Hephæstio which cost $1,200,000; and in Roman history we meet with similar instances. So, finally, the small bronze chariot exhumed from a tumulus in Mecklenburg recalls the wheeled structures fabricated for Solomon by Hiram of Tyre. (I. Kings, vii, 27–37.)

From time immemorial, civilized nations have recognized three ages in the history of society—the stone, bronze and iron ages. Archæology justifies this belief. In the stone age, the metals were unknown; in the bronze age, bronze displaced stone to some extent ; and in the iron age, iron came into use for cutting instruments. While these are the successive stages in the social development of peoples, they by no means serve as chronological landmarks for mankind at large; since different tribes and nations and races have passed out of their stone age at very different epochs, and many tribes still remain in their stone age. Researches have shown that the stone age must be sub-divided into three epochs :—the Palæolithic or Rude Stone Epoch, the Reindeer Epoch and the Neolithic or Polished Stone Epoch. In the first, human skill was very little developed, and man lived as contemporary with the mammoth, cave-bear, cave-hyena and other extinct quadrupeds, whose bones occur in caverns and river-drifts. In the Reindeer Epoch, human works were of a higher order; the animals just mentioned had chiefly disappeared, and the bones of the reindeer are most abundantly associated with human relics. In the Neolithic Epoch, stone weapons and implements were ground and polished, and some domestic animals had made their appearance.

The physical conditions of Europe on the first advent of the Stone Folk were strikingly different from the present. The continent was then just emerging from a secular winter which had buried all the mountains and plains beneath a mantle of glacier material as far south, probably, as the Pyrenees. England and Scandinavia had been connected with the continent; the English channel and the German ocean had been dry land, and the Thames had been a tributary of the Rhine. A subsidence now took place which made Great Britain an island. An amelioration of the climate caused a rapid melting of the glaciers; the land was extensively flooded and the drainage of the continent now began to mark out and to excavate the river valleys of the modern epoch. The cave-bear, mammoth and other quadrupeds of Pliocene time still survived; and now man appeared in Europe to dispute with them the possession of the forests and caverns. Now the swollen rivers flowed many feet above their present levels, and the relics of the Stone Folk were mingled with the deposits along their borders. The Reindeer Epoch witnessed another elevation and a new invasion of cold. England was again joined to the continent. The cave-bear and mammoth dwindled away. The reindeer and other northern quadrupeds were driven south over the plains of Languedoc and through the valleys of Perigord. The hyena went over to England and took possession of the caverns. But the men of Europe had made a slight advance in the industries. Next, another subsidence resulted in the isolation of England and the Scandinavian peninsula; the climate was again ameliorated, and the reindeer and other Arctic species retreated to Alpine elevations and northern latitudes. Now the modern aspects of the land began to appear, and now appeared various species of mammals destined to domestication—or, more probably, already domesticated in their oriental home. The ages of bronze, iron and authentic history succeeded.

It would, of course, be interesting to trace the physical, intellectual and moral characteristics of these primitive people in the light of the facts whose sources I have pointed out; but a brief article does not furnish the opportunity. A few words must suffice. *Physically* these people were of rather short stature, with roundish heads, and of a Mongoloid type, like modern Finns and Lapps. In the Neolithic epoch, they were not decidedly divergent from the Mediterranean race, while some of the skulls were equal in capacity to those of the very highest modern families. The Neanderthal skull, famous for its low forehead and massive brows, has a capacity of seventy-five cubic inches; and the Cro-Magnon skull a capacity of ninety-seven cubic inches *Socially* and *intellectually*, Palæolithic man existed in the rudest condition, ignorant even of the use of fire. In the Reindeer Epoch, he produced a better style of pottery, and was acquainted with fire. In the Neolithic Epoch cereals were cultivated and ground into flour; cloth was woven; bone combs were used; stores of fruit were preserved for winter's use; garden-tools were fashioned from stags' horns; log canoes were employed in navigation, and many other indications have been discovered of a fair inventive capacity and an extensive system of industries, even while yet every tool had to be constructed of stone, bone or stag's horn. *Esthetically* considered, the oldest Stone Folk had advanced no farther than the use of necklaces formed of shell beads. Some obscure etchings on stones exist. In the Reindeer Epoch, articles of ornament became decidedly abundant. *Religiously*, there is little to be affirmed or inferred of the Palæolithic tribes. Some curiously wrought flints may have served as religious emblems; and the occasional discovery of deposits of food near the body of the dead may very naturally be regarded as evidence of a belief in the future life. In the Reindeer Epoch, this class of evidences becomes very greatly augmented, as shown in the systematic and carefully provided burials in some of the tumulus-dolmens, and in the traces of funeral repasts in these and the rock-shelters of Aurignac, Bruniquel and Furfooz. The numerous specimens of bright and shining minerals found about many settlements may have been used as amulets, and may thus testify to the vague sense of the supernatural, which characterizes the infancy of human society. The Neolithic people add to such indications the erection of megalithic structures, some of which, surrounded by their cemeteries, as at Amesbury, England, must naturally be considered as their sacred temples.

Pre-historic man, in brief, represented, in Europe, the infancy of the human species. All his powers were undeveloped and uneducated. Every evidence sustains us in the conclusion that he was not inferior in psychic endowments to the average man of the highest races; but he was lacking in acquired skill, and in the results of experience accumulated through a long series of generations, and preserved from forgetfulness by the blessings of a written language.

This glance at the scientific facts bearing on the condition and physical relations of primeval man in Europe opens the way for a more intelligible discussion of the antiquity of the race at large.

CHAPTER VIII.

ANTIQUITY OF MAN.

The antiquity of the human species has generally been discussed from a point of view which I hold to be erroneous. It has almost always been assumed that when we have ascertained the antiquity of the oldest historic nations—the Egyptians and the Chinese—or, according to more recent views, of the Stone Folk of Europe, we have ascertained the antiquity of the human species. But, if the Black races are not descended from the progenitor of the White and Mongoloid races, these races are descended from the progenitor of the Black races, and possess an antiquity very much less than that of the Black races. The question, therefore, of the antiquity of the White race is quite different from that of the antiquity of the human species. The white man may have begun to exist six or eight thousand years ago; but the black man, I have reason to think, was thousands of years his predecessor upon the earth. The white man may have made his advent in central Asia; but the black man first appeared in Africa, or, more probably, upon an obliterated continent, of which the Mascarene Islands on the southeast of Africa are a surviving vestige. The first white man may have descended from a remote progenitor of black color; but the first black man could not have descended from a white progenitor.

The search for the antiquity of the human species is, therefore, a search for the antiquity of the Black races. That search must be instituted in the regions which the Black races have occupied —Africa, Australia and obliterated continental lands. These races have left no records, no monuments; and hence the search must become a purely geological one. This task is one which has never been undertaken; but it is one from which science will not shrink; and I anticipate that somewhere in the caverns of Abyssinia, or south Africa, or Australia, or in some of the stratified formations of those countries, we shall discover evidences of the existence of man at a date prior to the general glaciation of Europe and the United States.

For the present, however, we are compelled to restrict ourselves to an inquiry respecting the epoch of the oldest historic nations,

and of the prehistoric Stone Folk of Europe. Of the validity
of Chinese and Egyptian historic claims to a high antiquity I
shall express no opinion. I dissent emphatically, however, from
the position entertained by some recent archæologists, that the
Stone Folk of Europe carry us back fifty or a hundred thousand
years, or even that their antiquity is greater than that of the oldest historic nations. The opinion seems to me wild and fanatical.
The obscurity which hangs over the Stone Folk is mistakenly
ascribed to remoteness. Like objects seen in a fog, the events
of the Stone Age are not so remote as they seem. The latest
pile-habitations come down to the sixth. century. In many instances, the *debris* from the lacustrine villages has yielded Roman
coins and other works of Roman art. Homer's epic was composed
but 900 years before our era, and the Stone Folk were then in full
possession of central and northern Europe.

History declares that among the Lapps and Finns the Stone
Age descended to the time of Cæsar. The civilized Pelasgians
entered Greece 1400 years before Homer and found the Stone
Folk there. We have, then, at least twenty-five centuries of historical time for the duration of the Stone Age. I see no good
ground for the opinion that the primeval men of Europe appeared
more than 2500 or 3000 years before Christ. But, as a contrary
opinion is sometimes expressed, I will proceed to state the grounds
on which I understand it to be based, and then offer my reasons
for the rejection of these grounds.

I. *Pre-glacial remains of other animals have been mistaken for
human remains.* I refer to remains older than the continental
glacier of Europe. Some bones found at Saint Prest, France,
were observed to bear cuts and scratches which might have been
made by flint instruments in human hands. But with them were
associated the remains of a species of elephant, known to have
lived in later Pliocene time. Hence the mercurial Frenchman
made proclamation of *Pliocene man.* But actual experiment
proved that precisely similar markings are made upon bones by
the porcupine; and as a rodent left his bones in the same bed
with the cut and scratched bones, cooler reason promptly ascribed
the markings to rodent agency rather than human. Again, certain shell-marks near Bordeaux enclose the bones of a manatee.

which bear marks similarly ascribed to human agency. But the manatee lived in the Miocene period; therefore the Frenchman now proclaimed *Miocene man*. Unfortunately a fierce, carnivorous fish lived in the same waters, and was buried in the same cemetery, and his sharply serrated teeth exactly fit the markings on the scratched bones of the manatee. Tertiary man vanishes again. Finally at Thenay, again in France, some flints are found in lower Miocene limestone, which were at first pronounced the work of human hands. But bushels of similar flints may be picked up on any sea-beach of the chalk districts.

II. *Human remains erroneously supposed pre-glacial.* A human skeleton found in volcanic tuff at Le Puy-en-Velay, in central France, was associated with the bones of an elephant known to belong in Pliocene time. *Pliocene man* was again proclaimed, when, alas, some one showed that the elephant-bearing tuff was an *older* eruption than that bearing human bones, while the latter contained in fact the bones of another elephant—the well-known mammoth, which lived *after* the reign of ice. Again, the river drifts of the Somme were set down by the French geologists as pre-glacial or glacial in origin; and hence the flints which they enclose belonged to Tertiary man. The cooler heads of English geologists detected the fallacy, and pointed out several localities where it appears that even the valley of the Somme was not excavated till after the glacial drift was laid down; and the flint gravels are of still later date. In 1856 a human skull and numerous bones of the same skeleton were exhumed from the Calle del Vento in Liguria, and published to the world as "*l'uomo pliocenico;*" but no scientific observer saw the bones in place, and the best anthropologists now declare that the remains are not pliocene. A few years ago a sensation was created by the discovery of a human pelvis at Natchez, Mississippi, in a deposit of undoubted pre-glacial age. This, like all similar finds, filled the newspapers with sensational paragraphs calculated for the discomfiture of old opinions. But Sir Charles Lyell showed that the pelvis had in all probability fallen down from an Indian grave at the top of the bluff. So, from being a relic of pre-glacial man, it suddenly became the pelvis of a modern Cherokee, perhaps a hundred and fifty years old. The human remains of California, reported to be found under a sheet of Tertiary lava, are not sufficiently authenticated to form a subject of profitable discussion.

And this is all. These are the only evidences on which the claims of pre-glacial man in Europe have rested. But if he was post-glacial, what measure of years may express his antiquity? This is equivalent to asking the remoteness of the decline of the glacial epoch, which the Stone Folk certainly witnessed. The following are the grounds of the opinion, current to some extent, that fifty or a hundred thousand years separate us from the men who saw the decline of the continental glaciers.

I. *The astronomical hypothesis of glacial periods.* Recent astronomers have suggested that the glacial period was only the last of a succession, and that changes in astronomical conditions must produce such periods with calculable regularity. M. Adhemar has argued that the northern temperate zone must be glaciated once in 21,000 years by the influence of the precession of the equinoxes. Thus, the secular winter might be supposed to have passed about 10,500 years ago. But Mr. Croll, discrediting Adhemar, appeals to variations in eccentricity of the earth's orbit, and puts down 80,000 years as the time elapsed since maximum eccentricity led to continental glaciation. Accordingly, we might put the decline of the glaciers at 50,000 years ago, and this would indicate the antiquity of the Stone Folk. But I hold that archæology vetoes such a conclusion.

II. *Contemporaneousness of man with animals now extinct.* Geology once taught that all extinctions are remote in time; and hence, when man was found a contemporary with the mammoth and the cave bear, he was held to possess a high antiquity. But geology was mistaken. Extinctions have been recent. Extinctions are in progress. Continued extinctions are the order of nature. The Maories of New Zealand still retain traditions of the extinct gigantic birds of their islands. In Madagascar, the Dodo has lived within 250 years; but it is now extinct, like the solitaire and the Æpyornis. The huge *Rhytina gigas* has become extinct; as also the whale of the Bay of Biscay, which was once the basis of a flourishing industry. Other species are plainly approaching extinction. The Great Auk of Newfoundland has been seen but once in fifty years; and the Labrador Duck, ten years ago so abundant in the Fulton market, New York, has suddenly disappeared, and museums are bidding in vain for relics of the lost species. The Aurochs of Europe, abundant in Cæsar's time, is now saved from extinction only by the care of the Prussian government. The big trees of California will have no successors. In short, every species of animal which cannot occupy the continent with civilized man is clearly doomed to pass away. So extinctions continue, even in recent times, to be the order of nature.

III. *The magnitude of the geological changes since man's advent.* When we say that man was witness of the disappearance of the continental glacier in Europe, or learn that since his advent England and Scandinavia have been joined to the continent, and the North Sea has been dry land, and the Thames a tributary of the Rhine, we seem to sink back into geological time, where anything less than a hundred thousand years for man would be a ridiculous demand. So, too, when we learn that Mongoloid man came to America over an isthmus existing where Behring's Straits now are, and floated his canoe on the waters of a great lake, which spread over the prairie-region of Illinois.

But I believe, on sober reflection, that our imaginations have been excited. The mystery and the magnitude of geological changes seem to relegate them to the remote ages of convulsion and cataclysm. Let us not be frightened. We are in the midst of great changes, and are scarcely conscious of it. We have seen worlds in flames, and have felt a comet strike the earth. We have seen the whole coast of South America lifted up bodily ten or fifteen feet, and let down again in an hour. We have seen the Andes sink 220 feet in seventy years. We are pointed to vast hydrographical changes in China within historic times. As to the glaciers, they are still shrinking. Before our human eyes proceeds that retreat which has left its foot-prints all the way across the valley of Switzerland. We may still gaze on the ancient glaciers. We may still see them at their work. The Stone Folk are drawn down toward our own times. We look over the abyss of years and seize it in our apprehension. They saw the borders of the ice-field perhaps on the Rhine; we see them in Russia, and Siberia, and Greenland. And in our own country

6

their presence has been so recent that their stumps linger in the gulches of the Sierra Nevada; and huge masses remain undissolved in the ice-wells of Vermont, New York and Wisconsin. The truth is we are not so far out of the dust and smoke of antiquity as we had supposed. Antiquity is at our doors. Multitudes of facts might be cited which must tend to convince us that changes are in progress before our eyes, which must accomplish in a few thousand years results as great as those which separate the Stone Folk from us.

But how many years express the interval? This is the point on which it is not safe to be too precise. I can enumerate a dozen of the highest authorities in prehistoric archæology, who bring the epoch of polished stone down to within four to six thousand years of our time; and I could cite historical mention and historical data to show that the Stone Folk were known from a date 4000 or 5000 B. C., when the Iberians found them, down to 3000 or 3500 B. C., when the Iberian Libyans made war on Egypt, and thence down to 2000 B. C., when the Stone Folk were found in Sicily and Peloponnesus.

The Stone Folk had lived somewhere at an earlier epoch. Their Asiatic progenitors were more ancient. If descended from the white man's Adam, he must be removed somewhat further back than we have supposed. If Adam, however, is a divergent twig from the same stock as the Stone Folk, then the Stone Folk may have been in Europe even before our Adam appeared in Asia.

CHAPTER IX.

ORIGIN OF MAN.

The recognition of the descent from one stock, of types of structure as diverse as the European and the Australian, prompts at once an inquiry respecting the extent to which divergencies may have been carried. Whether the Negro has descended from the white man's Adam, or the Caucasian from the black man's Adam, there is implied a degree of physical divergence which is very suggestive of reflection. The more we insist on the blood affinity of the races of man, the more we crowd upon attention the query whether a blood affinity may not exist between the lowest race and some type of being a little too low to be called human.

The different races of men bear zoölogically such characteristics as would be employed to distinguish different species amongst the lower animals. I have heard the elder Agassiz declare that they differ as much as the different families of monkeys. Family distinctions are more profound than specific distinctions. If the various races of men are descended from a common stock, have we not as good grounds for assuming that the domestic dog, the prairie-dog, the wolf, the fox and the jackal are also descended from one stock? If parity of reasoning demands an affirmative response to this question, then the barriers are all down to admission of the derivative origin of organic forms in general. Now, while not affirming a parity of reasoning, it seems appropriate to state the grounds of derivative doctrine, preparatory to pointing out a disparity of an important kind. The general doctrine of the material continuity of organic forms seems to me to rest on the following classes of evidence :

I. *Analogical evidence.* Evolution is a law of thought, and hence a law of activity regulated by thought. An idea or concept is first grasped in its general character, then developed in detail. This is the method of the evolution of a sermon or a book. The longer thought dwells on the concept, the more there is evolved from it, under its general and subordinate divisions. This, however, is rather psychological than analogical evidence. But appropriate proof under this head is at hand. The method in the cosmos is a material continuity. Our earth has been what Jupiter is, and has been annulated like Saturn. It has been a sun, self-luminous; it is destined to become, as the moon, a fossil world. So our sun and all suns are in the midst of a progress of an identical kind. So the features of the earth's surface have become what they are through a continuous series of transitions from older to newer states—from less specialized to more specialized conditions. Again the succession of forms presented by a developing embryo is effected through a material continuity. The embryo retains its identity in passing through phases as diverse as a tadpole and an elephant—as diverse as a cell and a man.

11. *Geological evidence.* The forms of organization which have populated the world in its remote preparatory stages have been as diverse as the successive stages. Types of organization suited to a rude condition of the world demanded improvement when the conditions had improved. Fossil remains indicate that such improvements took place. It was not the displacement of the old type by the new, but a modification of the old type. So the general types of animals with which the world began to be populated in its infancy continue in existence If we take a particular existing type, as the proboscidian, we learn from the testimony of fossils, that it is a modification of a type which existed in the last geological age before the present. That was a modification of an older one, and that of a still older, and so on. If we take the existing type of ox, or hog, or horse, we discover in each case a series of older modifications of the type reaching back through Tertiary time. In the case of the horse the series of known forms is remarkably full. (See *Reconciliation of Science and Religion,* pp. 166-170.) Now these series of successions receding into the past constantly converge. That is, the ancient proboscidian type differed less from the hog or horse type than the modern one does. All the ancient types approximated each other. In some cases two or three types are found actually merged together. The judgment cannot resist the conviction that some distance farther back they all converge. Thus the modern types of mammals have diverged from a common five-toed, plantigrade, primitive form. But all this is no proof of genetic relationship in the terms of each series. All this might be if each term were a new beginning—an independent creation. This evidence is only a link in the proof.

III. *Variational evidence.* A species is now known not to be "a primordial organic form," as defined by Morton, but only a phase in a series of changes. That species vary to a wide extent has lately been shown by the study of many thousands of American birds. One-fourth of all our recognized species are only geographical varieties. The variations had become so wide that all naturalists recognized these varieties as good species. Something similar is true of our mammals. In short, it is now generally admitted that a large fraction of all hitherto recognized species are only varieties of certain forms which we must continue to admit as species. Some special instances of variation are quite striking. The axolotl of Colorado breathes water throughout life. But Dumeril, Prof. Marsh and others have caused this animal to absorb its gills and breathe air. It thus becomes a salamander. not only of a different species, but a different genus and tribe. So, certain marine crustaceans, gradually habituated to water less and less salt, undergo a transformation to fresh water species. By reversing the process, the transformation is reversed. It thus appears that transitions from one specific form to another are in the order of nature, and we learn that the transition from one modification of the horse type to another, during the lapse of Tertiary time, is a solution of the problem of successional forms which may be legitimately contemplated. The genetic relation of one term to another is not in conflict with nature, but is now strongly suggested by the aptitude of organic forms to vary.

IV. *Embryological evidence.* Every embryo in its course of development passes, by continuity, through a succession of stages, beginning with a cell. My limited space forbids to particularize, but I may state that the human embryo exhibits not fewer than twenty-two stages pretty distinctly marked, each in succession more complicated than the preceding ones. Now the points to be made in view of embryonic stages are the following: 1. The embryonic stages of all animals are, to a certain extent, *identical*. The simplest animals pass through but few of these stages; higher animals more. 2. Embryonic stages furnish a parallelism with the *gradations* of existing animals. The lowest animals having gone through three or four stages are arrested and live as permanent representatives of the last stage reached. Animals successively higher pass through successively more of the stages, and, becoming arrested, stand permanently as pictures of the highest embryonic stages reached. So the gradation of animal forms in the world becomes a series parallel with the series exemplified by the embryonic history of every higher animal. 3. Embryonic stages furnish parallels with the geological succession. That is, the succession of types of animals in geological time presents the same characters and the same order as the embryonic history of any higher vertebrate.

Now the embryonic succession is a demonstrated continuity. Is not the identical succession revealed by palæontology also a continuity? If the analogy does not convince, the aptitude to variation predisposes to conviction; and conviction becomes almost irresistible, when we reflect that a profound similarity—indeed, a physiological identity—obtains between the mode of the continuity in embryonic and genealogical successions. I can do scarcely more than enunciate conclusions; and I fear the reader will wonder, at the end, what is the evidence on which they rest.

Now, we may admit the force of the evidence, and still, with Wallace, hesitate to admit that the body and soul of man fall under the law of evolution; or, with Miyart, admit the principle with reference to the human body, and deny it with reference to the human soul. 1. A great gap exists between man and all other animals. Structurally, his brain and cranium as much surpass an ape's as an ape's surpass an eel's. Psychically, man is equally differentiated from the highest brute. 2. No connecting links between man and the brutes are known. In the living world the fact is patent. In the extinct world we should expect to discover forms immediately below man, but they are not forthcoming. We find neither connecting links nor remains certifying to such antiquity as man must possess, if a derived form. On the whole, the question in reference to man is quite open. We are very far from the possession of evidence that his organism has been evolved; still farther from the proof that his soul is derived from the psychic nature of a brute.

I express myself simply as a scientist. As such, I warn the reader not to be disturbed by any conclusions of science either achieved or impending. It is absolutely immaterial whether God created man by a fiat instantly, or by a fiat derivatively. Whether man has been evolved or not, he is the work of a Creator; and every moment's continuance of his being is a manifestation of power so far superior to the prerogatives of matter as to constitute an ever-repeated creation. There has been a great deal of dogmatism in science, and it is as much to be deprecated as dogmatism in religion. Science is progressive, and it is not the sign of a well ballasted intelligence to be moved with apprehension over any fresh utterance of science. Every theory must be subjected to appropriate tests. If it stands, it becomes a new revelation of God's mind; if it falls, all our trepidation over the supposed consequences becomes ridiculous.

At the meeting of the German Association for the Advancement of Science, last summer at Munich, Professor Hæckel, of Bonn, delivered a lecture in which he indulged in some of his characteristic sneering at spiritualism, and clinched his positions with the customary self-asserting dogmatism. To this lecture fitting reference was made by Professor Virchow, of Berlin, an older, more candid and abler investigator in the same field; and I close by a citation from Virchow's address.

"All attempts to transform our problems into doctrines, to introduce our theories as the bases of a plan of education, [as Hæckel had proposed,] particularly the attempt simply to depose the Church, and to replace its dogma by a religion of descent, these attempts, I say, must fail. Therefore, let us be moderate; let us exercise resignation, so that we give even the most treasured problems which we put forth, always as problems only, and that we say it a hundred and again a hundred times: Do not take this for confirmed truth—be prepared that, perhaps, this may be changed....Only ten years ago, when a skull was found, perhaps in peat, or in lake dwellings, or in some old cave, it was believed that marks of a wild and quite undeveloped state were seen in it. Indeed, we were then scenting monkey-air; but this has died out more and more....But I must say that one fossil monkey skull or man ape skull which really belonged to a human proprietor has never been found. We cannot teach, we cannot designate it as a revelation of science, that man descends from the ape, or from any other animal."

CHAPTER X.

PATRIARCHAL CHRONOLOGY.

In assuming the position that the Black races are Preadamites I have depended chiefly on the two following propositions: 1. The time from Adam (according to accepted chronology) to the date at which we know the Negro type had been fully established is vastly too brief for so great a divergence, in view of the imperceptible amount of divergence since such date. 2. No amount of time would suffice for the divergence of the Black races from the white man's Adam, since that would imply degeneracy of a racial and continental extent, and this is contrary to the recognized principle of progress in nature. At the same time I have *assumed* that the Mongoloid and Dravidian races may have descended from our Adam, both because the divergence in these cases is comparatively slight, and because those races, intellectually and morally, stand nearly on a level with our own. But I have not been *satisfied* with this assumption respecting the Brown races, because I do not think the Usher chronology affords sufficient time even for such a degree of differentiation. I admit the possibility; but I feel that the assumption is a strain upon the evidence.

What we need, then, to relieve us of this difficulty, is more time between Adam and the dawn of written history; and especially between Adam and the Deluge. But this is only one phase of the ethnological data which would be greatly accommodated and relieved by a larger allowance of time. The fourth chapter of Genesis, for instance, appears to have been composed before the Deluge—perhaps in the 500th year of Noah (Gen. v. 32); but at that time there were peoples in existence, descended from Cain, who were celebrated for agriculture, mechanics and music. They were indeed descended from Jabal, Jubal and Tubal-Cain, of the eighth generation from Adam. But, as the ten generations from Adam to the 500th year of Noah cover only 1,526 years, we may assume the eight generations to Tubal-Cain to cover about 1,245 years; and hence from Tubal-Cain to the 500th year of Noah we have only about 300 years, which is insufficient time, in the infancy of the world, for the growth of tribes and nations and culture which seem then to have been in existence.

Take another case. The tenth chapter of Genesis narrates a series of events which took place after the flood and before the division of the land in the time of Peleg. Computing the time in the usual way, the interval from the flood to the birth of Reu, the son of Peleg, was 131 years; and, according to the usual rate of increase, the posterity of Noah must have amounted to about 900 persons. This chapter was written in the time of Peleg, as otherwise the history would have been brought down to a later

date, as it is in the eleventh chapter. But note the progress
which had been made in the settlement of the world and the
building of cities, at the date of this composition. The posterity
of Japhet had moved westward and taken possession of the
islands of the Ægean and the Mediterranean, and probably the
adjacent continental regions, and had spread over the vast territory of Scythia on the north, and penetrated to Spain on the west.
They had become separated into distinct "languages, families
and nations." This is a glimpse of ethnic events which we cannot reasonably assume to have taken place in 131 years. Again,
the descendants of Ham had accomplished even greater results.
Egypt had been settled, and its population had become differentiated into at least eight tribes or nations. Phœnician Sidon had
been built and the Phœnicians had grown into nine peoples, "and
afterward the families of the Canaanites spread abroad." But
before the Canaanites there were present in Palestine the Rephaim,
Zuzim, Emim and others. Who were these peoples? Nimrod,
also, or his posterity, had planted cities. Babel, Erech, Accad
and Calneh were the "*beginning* of his kingdom." Then Asshur
arose amongst the Nimrodites and led away a colony, which built
other walled cities—Nineveh, Rehoboth, Calah, and Resen which
was "a great city." Thus the descendants of Ham had developed
"families and tongues and countries and nations." The posterity
of Shem also had become divided into "families and tongues and
nations" and dispersed to many "lands." Accordingly the descendants of Noah, in the days of Peleg, had become numerous
"nations" and divided the earth amongst themselves. Now it is
difficult to believe that these cities and nationalities had come into
existence from one family in the space of 131 years.

A similar set of considerations is furnished by the eleventh
chapter, which seems to be a distinct document, and begins back
at an epoch near the flood, and preserves the history down to
Abraham. Journeying westward, the Adamites, as yet one family,
attempted to build a tower, and were defeated. Still, it appears
a city known as Babel rose into existence, and it would be fair to
presume that this and the other cities named as the beginning of
Nimrod's kingdom, instead of being built by him or his successors, were already in existence long before the time of Nimrod.

7

How much, then, beyond 131 years must the time from Noah to Peleg be elongated ?

These are simply samples of the exigencies which arise on biblical, ethnological, scientific and linguistic grounds, when we make the attempt to satisfy ourselves with the popular chronology. I think, therefore, I shall do my readers a service by directing their attention to a recent work which undertakes to show that the original text of Genesis, when rightly understood, gives us a much more extended chronology. The work is written by Rev. T. P. Crawford, of Fung Chow, China, and published in Richmond, Virginia, by Josiah Ryland & Co., and is entitled " The Patriarchal Dynasties from Adam to Abraham shown to cover 10,500 years, and the highest human life only 187." The fundamental position assumed by the author is a reformed reading of the genealogical tables contained in the fifth and eleventh chapters of Genesis ; of which the first traces the posterity of Adam to Noah, and the second traces the posterity of Noah to Abraham. For the purpose of giving an intelligible explanation of Mr. Crawford's reformed reading, I here reproduce the biblical paragraph touching the family of Adam :

" And Adam lived a hundred and thirty years, and begat *a son* in his own likeness, after his image ; and called his name Seth. And the days of Adam after he had begotten Seth were eight hundred years ; and he begat sons and daughters : And all the days that Adam lived were nine hundred and thirty years ; and he died."

A similar paragraph is recorded respecting each of the antediluvian patriarchs. Now the author maintains that the word Adam is employed, above, in a *personal*, and afterward in a *family*, sense ; that the first clause denotes *the whole life* of Adam, and not his age at the birth of Seth ; that *yolad*, translated " begat," signifies rather " appointed," and refers to Adam's designation of Seth (in place of Abel) to be his successor ; that " likeness " and " image " refer not to personal appearance, but to character and office—the name Seth itself signifying " The appointed ; " that " Adam " in the next clause refers to the tribe or family of Adam ; that the Adamic family continued to be ruled over by successors not in the line of Seth, for a period of 930 years ; that thereafter the

representatives of the Sethite line acceded to the kingship for
912 years, when the family of Enos assumed the government, and
so on.

These positions are argued with much ability. That the first
clause expresses the whole life of Adam is maintained on the following grounds: 1. The Hebrew never employs the verb *lived*
with definite numbers to indicate the age of a man at the birth of
a son; but it invariably says such a one *was a son* of so many
years *when* his son was born, or some other event took place.
Many passages are cited, of which see Gen. xxi, 5; xvi, 16; xvii,
24; xxi, 4; Lev. ix, 3; Josh. xiv, 7; I. Kings xiv, 21; xx, 42.
On the contrary, the verb *lived* denotes the whole term of a man's
life.   See Gen. i, 22; xxiii, 1; xxv, 7; xlvii, 28; v, 5; xi, 11; ix,
28; II. Kings xiv, 17; Job xliii, 16.   2. Antediluvian life is sub-
stantially asserted to have been one hundred and twenty years, on
an average. (See Gen. vi, 3.) 3. There is nowhere in the Old
Testament any allusion to such enormous ages as eight hundred
and nine hundred years.   On the contrary, Abraham, who was
promised a "good old age," died at one hundred and seventy-five
years. (Gen. xv, 15; xxv, 7, 8.)   So Isaac, at one hundred and
eighty years, was "old and full of days," (Gen. xxxv, 28, 29.)
Other reasoning I have not the space to cite.   A paraphrase of
the paragraph concerning Adam would, therefore, read somewhat
as follows:

And Adam lived a hundred and thirty years.   And at the close
of his life he appointed his son to be his spiritual heir and successor and designated him Seth, "The appointed."   And the
duration of the house of Adam after the appointment of Seth
was eight hundred years, represented by male and female descendants.   And the whole duration of the house of Adam was
nine hundred and thirty years, and it ceased to exist.

The paragraphs touching the other antediluvian patriarchs are
to be similarly understood.   It will thus appear that the average
duration of life was then one hundred and twenty years.   A similar interpretation of the eleventh chapter gives the average duration of life after the flood at one hundred and twenty-eight.
After Abraham, the ages, as stated in the sacred text, range from
one hundred and ten to one hundred and eighty years, with an

average of one hundred and thirty-five years. Still further, the utmost limit of ancient Egyptian life was one hundred and ten years. The average life of the eight kings of the second Chaldean dynasty was eighty-eight years. Under the first Chinese dynasty of four hundred and thirty-nine years, average life was seventy-seven years; under the second, of six hundred and forty-four years, it was sixty-nine years. These two dynasties extended from the days of Peleg to those of Solomon. Many other facts tend to show that human life, in the most ancient times, had a duration not far from that of the Hebrew patriarchs, if we interpret the first clause of each paragraph as proposed by Mr. Crawford; while the marvelous duration of human life, according to the popular interpretation, is opposed to every item of knowledge which we possess from other sources.

Applying these principles to the genealogical tables of Genesis, we obtain the following chronological data:

Adam to the flood.......	7,737 years
Flood to the birth of Abraham.............................	2,763 "
Adam to Abraham............... ...:.....................	10,500 "
Birth of Abraham to Christ......................	2,000 "
Adam to Christ..	12,509 "
Christ to the present time................................	1,878 "
Adam to the present year..................................	14,378 "

It is to be hoped that Hebrew scholars will give Mr. Crawford's views a candid examination, and I will also indulge the hope that they may find his exegesis valid.